Praise for *London Triptych*

'Charting three very different affairs taking place against the backdrop of three very different Londons, Jonathan Kemp's first novel is a thought-provoking enquiry into what changes in gay men's lives as the decades pass – and what doesn't. This is a book that will make you think – and make you feel.'
Neil Bartlett

'What an amazing book. This is the best gay novel to be published in many years. It is literary fiction at its best.'
Clayton Littlewood

'Despite reaching across a century, Kemp's characters are believable and down-to-earth; the focus is not on period setting but on dialogue. A thoroughly absorbing and pacy read... a fresh angle on gay life and on the oldest profession.'
Time Out

'London itself, in its relentless indifference, is as powerful a presence here as the three gay men whose lives it absorbs.'
Times Literary Supplement

'The three stories explore a subculture and an underworld that is hidden from the everyday, yet whilst they are historically and socially distinct tales each one echoes a universal experience. As a writer Jonathan Kemp is akin to the Pied Piper, if only because there is something magical you cannot help but follow.'
Polari

'By turns explicit and energetic, Kemp's forceful prose uncompromisingly draws the reader in. A strange, squalid, rather interesting book.'
Metro

'The patchwork crossover of lives and destinies is explored with a voice that sometimes reminded me of Alan Hollinghurst and other times soared into the metaphorically agonised realms of Elizabeth Smart. l   d.'

'A dark novel about exploitation and betrayal that's full of rent boys, aristos and artists. That's got to beat the new Marian Keyes any day, right?'
Boyz Magazine

'From living outside the law to living outside the society, times are irrelevant when it comes to the sentiment of gay men: one of turmoil, of irretrievable loss, of struggle over stigma, and of unrequited love. *London Triptych* captures these political and emotional battles with a lyrical beauty and raw lucidity.'
A Guy's Moleskine Notebook

'First-time novelist Kemp's book is an intriguing look at the homosexual experience through the prism of male prostitution over the past 100 years.'
Hackney Hive

'Not only a devastatingly honest exposé of our hidden gay past, but a heartbreaking examination of the intricacies of the gay psyche. Above all, this is a story about the power of feeling and the hope and beauty that can be found in even the darkest places.'
Dissident Musings

'*London Triptych* is, hands down, the most heart-wrenching and profound piece of literature I have read this year.'
Pink Sheep Café

'The three characters and stories showed the differences in the years but also gave voice, masterfully, to those normally silenced. Kemp shows that the way we see the world is not actually necessarily the way it is or the way that others see it.'
Amy Says

'Kemp has achieved what few writers ever will, a work that stands alone as a heartbreaking love letter not only to a vast and fascinating place, but also to the lives within that serve as its beating heart.'
Gaydarnation

To read an extract from **London Triptych**, *turn to p.123*

26

Jonathan Kemp

Myriad Editions

First published in 2011 by
Myriad Editions
59 Lansdowne Place
Brighton BN3 1FL

www.MyriadEditions.com

1 3 5 7 9 10 8 6 4 2

A CIP catalogue record for this book is available
from the British Library.

ISBN: 978-0-9567926-0-0

Printed on FSC-accredited paper by
CPI Group (UK) Ltd, Croydon, CR0 4YY

For Roy Woolley

'However much men may shudder,
philosophy must say everything.'

~ *Marquis de Sade*

'He who wishes to know the truth
about life in its immediacy must
scrutinize its estranged form.'

~ *Theodor W. Adorno*

'Only in darkness can men truly
be themselves, and therefore night
is holier than day.'

~ *Michelangelo*

This is for all those nights filled with pleasure and oblivion; for all those hours spent wandering the maze of other men's bodies, as if you were crawling the deck of a sinking galley;

This is for all the ones who cry out when they come, and for the ones who don't because they know that sometimes it's just sexier that way, making the gasps go inwards like blue smoke;

This is for all those who find themselves on their knees at nine p.m. in a small park in this city of wounded boys and sexual warriors, barely hidden by bushes, sucking off a man in white trackies who told his girlfriend he was going for a jog (you know who you are); for all those who love it when he leans over to retrieve his beer can without breaking the stride of his wank; the way he slugs it back, fist still pumping;

This is for when the blood turns black and burns you from the inside, for when you get the hunger — feel it unravelling within its long, dark spine of want; for when the only thing to do is go out and seek what you need in that place where the shadows grow as you pass through them, like a woman strolling through a cloud of perfume she has just released before her;

This is for then, for those crystalline moments when your body moulds to your desires, contoured by the red heat of longing, and fuelled by all the imaginings you hold.

For when no truth could be less secure.

Aa

We spend the night exchanging handwritten notes, using a pad and pen the barman has supplied, you writing words you have never spoken, will never speak. Your writing is spidery as a child's first efforts. I wish I'd kept them, those marks on paper which form a loop that binds us and pulls us back to my flat where we undress in silence and haste in my candlelit bedroom.

And I am not prepared at all for the sounds that rip out of you when you come, the death rattle of pleasure, more bestial than human, which pierce the room like a gaggle of bats bursting into the night sky from the dark recess of a cave and filling it with Minerva's screeches; from your cock is released a flock of snow-white doves. Trained in silence, locked in speechlessness, you are unschooled, untamed, letting go of sounds as you let go of your orgasm, in violent bursts that tear like an incision in flesh. Then you sink back into a big-grinned muteness that says everything there is to say about what we have just shared.

These sounds you give to articulate your pleasure are far removed from the discreet insistencies of language.

I snap at the darkness and swallow them like a bird plucking flies from the air. I too want to give up these sounds from a body rendered voiceless by language. I too want to tear myself open and release something monstrous and wild, something from the other side of language, where reason lies comatose and pointless.

Bb

I ring the doorbell three times as arranged.

The door release clicks and I push the door open and enter the building. I make my way up to the first floor and the door to the flat is open, as arranged.

The flat is in darkness, but for an ultraviolet glow from the bedroom. I enter to find a naked man face-down on the bed.

He sits up, picks up a joint from the bedside cabinet and lights it, taking a long, slow pull before handing it over to me. I unfasten my trousers and step closer towards him before taking the joint. He slides his hand through my open fly and plays with my cock through the fabric of my jockstrap. The wind through the open window makes the blind throw itself against the glass in gatling fits.

'Nice one,' he says as he feels my cock stiffen under his touch. I push my jeans down and he pulls my cock out and slides his mouth onto it; I groan and lean across to place the joint in an ashtray before peeling off my T-shirt. The man takes a sniff of poppers and hands the bottle to me. My nervous system crackles in nitrous blue flashes as I reflect on the brain cells I'm killing, feeling each one pop like a blown light bulb in my skull.

He sucks all the way down to the root, right down to the metal of my cock ring and the universe becomes a place I can live in once more.

I spiral with pleasure, sliding along the curves of the spiral till I land in the centre with a splash. I push him back onto the bed and climb above, thrusting into his face with my hips. He moans with pleasure as I feed him, as arranged. Grunts erupt from my throat with each release. He swallows every drop. I slide out and slide my body down across his till my chin rests on the top of his shaved head and I stay like that for a moment, feeling just enough tenderness to consider planting a kiss on his crown, and just enough restraint to hold back. I roll over onto my back next to him, recovering from the high, floating back into my body from the white light of orgasm. 'Fuck, that was hot.'

'It certainly was,' he says, licking his lips and sitting up to get a cigarette. My fingertips glow from the UV, emitting their own light. As I look at them I wonder what it could possibly signify, this feral hunger that pushes me towards this.

Does it signify anything at all?

During the long walk home these words emerge like bubbles and I write them down for someone to read, someone like you.

He has five more men due to visit him throughout the night.

Cc

At three a.m., at the back of Jack Straw's Castle, a fissure opens up in reality, through which he steps, and a new world unfolds beneath his feet; the trees grow denser with each step, the air more primitive and wild. He looks across the tree-tops and beyond to a sky the colour of which remains nameless, knowing that this night will never leave him. On his deathbed this memory will visit him like a nursing angel. The timeless landscape matches the timeless feeling inside. The wind gets tangled in the tops of the trees. The night races forward like a dark horse. Fear and desire commingle within the swinging pendulum of his stomach. The distinctive sound of a slap against bare flesh flaps through the air towards him.

'Come on,' his friend whispers excitedly, grabbing his arm, breaking the reverie, 'there's someone at the Spanking Tree.'

The two friends move quickly through a shadowed clump of trees, where men lean and loiter, others passing slowly by, skirting close enough to make out the value of the chase. Now and then a cigarette tip burns red against the black, or a lighter flame momentarily pulls a face from out of the dark.

They emerge in a clearing, in the centre of which lies a fallen tree, its trunk worn to a bare polish, its branches withered or broken. A naked man lies across the curve of the trunk, and in the half-light they can make out his moonwhite buttocks. Another man is standing beside him, bringing his palm down in slowly paced smacks that ripple through the silence. A group of men forms around them: hands moving across bodies, cocks emerging from flies, mouths meeting mouths. Outside the circle, a daddy bear stands holding his boy's black leather jacket. He is big and round and white-bearded, Santa Claus in faded denim. His boy stands tall and lean and smoothly white amidst the pack, jeans puddled at his feet, white T-shirt rucked behind his head. Several men kneel before him, taking it in turns to suck him. The two friends approach, have their go and move on. Daddy walks over and whispers something to his cub and the young boy lifts his jeans and lowers his T-shirt and they walk away, to start somewhere else. Two or three men follow, dancing to his tune, cruising to the sweet smell of this naked climate.

The darkness moves like a vapour, coagulating around bodies – only to evaporate in their heat. As the two friends move silently on one of them spots someone and, grabbing the other by the wrist, pulls him towards new prey. He approaches a tall, well-built skinhead, whispers something to him. The words disappear, lost forever. The three men move off towards some bushes,

14

unlocatable now, without those maps that have yet to be drawn. Tucked into a space behind a tree, the two friends kneel before the skinhead's porn-star cock, passing the amyl and taking it in turns to choke and sniff, choke and sniff. The skinhead lets loose a stream of verbal in rough cockney: 'Look at him demeaning himself, sucking on that fascist cock with his nigger lips. You like that big fascist cock, don't you, you filthy cocksucking queer.' The two friends will laugh about this later, but for now they are hungry so they feed, passing the cock between them, each enjoying watching the other go to work. Sharing it brings something to the act that, had only one of them been present, would be missing. A thrill, a joy, an intimacy it would be impossible to try to name or describe. They push their faces forward and open their mouths in unison when the skinhead says he is about to come, and receive the blessing as their just reward. In this world they have entered, this drink is the only nutrition. Like extracting the sap from rare fruits, they will move from tree to tree for hours, sometimes finding nothing, sometimes a feast.

On their way out, the man selling drinks and poppers from a bench near the car park will ask, 'Had yer Weetabix, lads?'

Driving out of the car park as the sun begins to rise, they will pass a short, stocky, hairy man squeezed into a blue-sequinned mini-dress, rocking on black kitten heels, his big fuzzy arms swinging by his side, off to taste the freedom only found in this other world, and then only rarely. The night folds up like a sheet of paper, sliding itself into their memories, to be unfolded and relived, recounted and treasured.

Sometimes life isn't meant to make sense.

Dd

Or that time when I awoke to the rhythm of you fucking me, taking me, pulling me by the waist towards you, slamming against me, me slamming against you as I rise into consciousness like a swimmer breaking the surface, breathless and disorientated, locating myself, drowning in sensation. The darkness and the pillow and you inside me like fireworks. I know I'll never know that night again. Nor that brutal love that's locked within my blood.

The projector jams, the screen blistering into white light as the celluloid disintegrates and the scene dissolves. I disintegrate and the scene dissolves.

Or that time in the cemetery one hot summer afternoon, sheltered only by the thin curtain of greenery growing over the doorway we have joined within, your body in my body, locked in some secret pact that pushes us together, as if our only hope of salvation is to merge into one single creature, my shorts round my knees, my bare skin brushed by brickdust, my love for you immeasurable.

Or that time on the roof, both naked, draped in summernight heat, the city spinning around us like a ring of meteors which satellites the planet our bodies have made. Circling us, the universe expands its star-flecked possibilities, and Heaven rains down, not thunderbolts, but flowers, that fall on us and about us in bursts of colour.

These moments tear at me, clawing for attention. My body is a book overflowing with stories that can't be read without your hands roaming the Braille of my sensations.

The possibility of using our bodies as a source of very numerous pleasures is something that is very important. Sexuality is part of our behaviour, part of our freedom, something that we ourselves create. It is our creation, and much more than the discovery of a secret side of our desire. With it we make and unmake the world. With it, we speak a different tongue.

Ee

The communication joining lovers depends on the nakedness of their laceration. Their love signifies that neither can see the being of the other but only a wound and a need to be ruined. And no greater desire exists than a wounded person's need for another wound.

All attempts at joy are futile but necessary, like everything we do. But it is not until we are out of the dark that we can assess the extent of the damage. The doorbell rings, and we run down to the hallway in our underpants, giggling like children. As the skunk wends its way through the burrows of my mind, I feel desire uncoil within like a bullwhip, lashing out at the world to see what it can fell.

He had wanted us naked when he arrived, but we compromised with underwear.

He had wanted us on our knees, so, after turning the key and pulling the door slightly ajar, I fall to my knees, the consummate act of submissive worship. Erotic submission is a limit-experience, beyond which something else comes into play, something not quite human. It all happens so quickly, and time slows down only once it has passed. The organic flows of the body – sperm, blood, piss and shit – are conducive to the amorphous manifestations of corporeal pleasure. The human body shatters beneath a multiplicity of sensations and intensities the overall experience of which results in what has been erroneously called 'the subject'. My question is this: can the movements and flows of the body be represented, or does representation itself only function upon a foreclosure of such nomadic flesh?

F f

As much as language threatens the body, however, the body also threatens language.

The music is loud, guitar-based, rock pop. The space in front of the stage where earlier a band had played is now scattered with people dancing. In the centre of the crowd, stripped to the waist, his lean body hairless and slick with sweat, this lupine man whirls inside the unpredictable steps of St Vitus. He unbuttons his flies and lets his baggy jeans slink to the floor, revealing his cock. He moves too fast, too manic, for anyone to do anything but watch. His head is an explosion of dark thick curls, his face all Caravaggio hunger and intensity. I have barely articulated to myself how much I want him when he is pulling up his jeans and tearing through the crowd towards me: a cannonball in human form. He fells me and we crawl and roll like wrestlers in the beer-mud that covers the bare wood floor. I manage to fight loose and stand up only to be floored once more, this time pushed backwards onto an empty couch against the wall. He lands with a belly flop that momentarily winds me. I am dizzy with lust and confusion. His warm wet skin is under my hands, his hands are on me, one down the front of my jeans, squeezing my cock. 'I've got a big thick Irish cock,' he drawls warmly in my ear in his rich Dublin brogue, 'I know what you boys like.' Through the haze of the drink and the speed of the encounter, I look past the boy's shoulder to see a barman standing watching us, terrified and unsure what to do. The boy kisses me, hard and urgently, and the lights on the ceiling kaleidoscope wildly. The music allows me to imagine this isn't happening in reality; it is only my wishes assaulting me. My booze-sodden imagination has created something that seems real, the way a dream can when you inhabit it, but dissolves once you crawl from the damp cave of sleep. I slide my hand down the back of his jeans and take in the firm round perfection of his arse, the blunt suede hardness of his coccyx. His skin beneath my palm is hot and wet. The barman invades this Eden in which we lie and says, 'Oi, lads, pack it in, will you?' I don't feel any danger, only the hot hot heat of the immediate, and this loud bright crazy music seems to be the only voice I hear.

Outside, in the street, he presses a white pill into my mouth and kisses me again, and I wash it down with a mixture of his boozy spittle and mine. 'Wanna go to a party?' he asks, and soon we are transported into a house nearby, where about a dozen people are sitting drinking, listening to The Clash. He tells me his name is Niall. His handsome face is mischief. We have some MDMA in the bathroom and kiss some more, before returning to the lounge, where he collapses on the sofa and sinks into a deep sleep. I decide to stay. My head is packed with energy and possibility. My mind is a staircase up which I am frantically running. I talk and dance the whole night through with these strangers who share with me their drugs and their music and their laughter; and just before sunrise Niall stirs and stands and takes me by the hand and leads me out into the sun-sugared streets of morning like a guardian angel. Birds are singing all around us, their notes dipping and soaring like bubbles popping. I know what hands are for and I'd like to help myself. This line goes round and round in my disconnected head as he leads me by the hand to a squat in Hackney, where he warms up some lentil soup which we share before going to his room. It is a high-ceilinged whitewashed room. The floor is littered with clothes, a mattress in one corner, stacks of records all around, piles of books, a Lloyd Loom chair. A mannequin sprayed silver stands by the window, its neck laden with gold chains, on its head a purple beehive wig. When he is naked I notice something I had not seen in the club. Now, in the grey daylight that breaks through the white sheet hung up against the window, I can see the letters standing out in legible scars across his hairless chest. D-E-N-I-A-L. For the briefest moment I love this wounded man/boy, in whose eyes I see the recognisable burn of drugs and sex and hunger. He shines with a lost need, a lonely greedy fucked-up cock-sure need and we fall against each other and onto that grimy mattress. We lie, head to toe, feeding on each other's cocks. I occupy every last space available for this experience, I inhabit this feeling of pleasure, wanting it never to end. And that word, DENIAL, plays across the black expanse of my consciousness, repeats and repeats, like a broken record, and I want to know what it means, why it is there, who did it to him, or did he do it to himself? The letters are sharp and clear, rising like Braille, seeming to crave touch to be complete. Too steady to have been done by his own hand, perhaps. I want to ask him, but I don't. Instead, I let the tension gather up and disperse into the unravelled moment of my orgasm, let the hot cum he has just shot across my neck and chest turn to cold water and run down to the dirty sheets before I say, 'Have you got a towel, mate?'

After wiping ourselves down, we fall into a spoon, him inside the naked Z of my folded body, and I can feel the need for sleep enter my muscles. I think about what it takes to cut words into skin, what it feels like, the warm fluid oozing, the intense pain, the gathering and releasing of the body's forces, the chaos inside that translates into those six skinwhite letters. I wonder what it must be like to share your life with a man like that, realising – with a deep deep sadness made worse by the drugs and lack of sleep – that it wouldn't, couldn't, make my loneliness diminish or my loss decrease.

Gg

s it speech that holds the truth, or silence? Is it through words that I will know you, or through grunts, sighs, gasps and mews? I tried to hold you in my hands, but you were too big, too elusive. I tried to keep a grip on things, but love got in the way.

Your body, to me, was like an altar and my piety knew no bounds. I drank your piss like Holy wine, and believed, and believed, and believed.

Your body, to me, was like a miracle, to be awed by again and again. I said your name in my waking hours like a prayer, and wished more than anything that things could have been different.

If my body means anything to you now, it is only in dreams, like a ghost, that it appears. The thought of you is a wave breaking violently on the shore of my consciousness, merciless and cruel. To this question – the question of our bodies, together – there can never be an answer, only an endless retelling of the question to complete strangers.

Hh

What desire can be against nature since it was given to man by nature? Across town, Alan is sitting naked on his toilet with a massive black rubber dildo jammed up his well-lubed arsehole, a bottle of poppers in his right hand from which he sniffs furiously at each stab of pain, like an asthmatic inhaling to assuage an attack. He has decided that he wants to get fisted and is trying to stretch himself in preparation. Over the weeks he has been progressing to bigger and bigger dildos. The diameter of the dildo now halfway inside his rectum is a good six inches. He is in agony, his cock shrivelled to nothing with the shock to his nerves. His head crackles black like a wartime wireless. He cannot understand why his sphincter refuses to ease and allow more of the black rubber to penetrate. His head swims with sounds like bells chiming, and just as he pulls on the dildo instead of pushing, trying to ease it out, he collapses, unconscious. He comes around face-down on the cold tile floor, his arse in the air, the small brown bottle still gripped in his fist, and an acute pain ripping up the centre of his back. He looks at his watch: twenty minutes have passed. This must be what it is like giving birth, he thinks, gently climbing back onto the toilet seat. I am giving birth to pleasure, to submission, to the destruction of my 'self'; I am enabling the body to fragment and the fragments to circle around the central column of a destabilised subjectivity, like gulls riding a thermal. I am coaxing that tricky little muscle to do something it doesn't want to do. I am dominating myself, sodomising myself, raping my body's own desire for unity, storming the citadel of my sovereignty with the battering ram of madness.

But if you could just see the beauty, there are things I could never describe. This is the thing I have prayed for; this is my unbroken prize.

It is only by being 'unnatural' that one recovers from one's naturalness, from one's lack of spirituality.

He said: 'Making love is such an entire negation of isolated existence that we find it natural, even wonderful in a sense, that an insect dies in the consummation it sought out.'

He wrote: 'Begging on all fours to be fucked up the arse in the name of progress is the only authentic expression of humanity.'

He sang: 'You will know nothing unless you have known everything.'

Right now, as my body splinters beneath your will, his words become dermagraphics that rotate on the surface of my skin, or rather not on the surface but just underneath the first layer, like solid objects pushing their sharp particularity through the tissuey membrane and making the sensations assailing me comprehensible, locatable, though only just, for they never become single discrete units, but rather form a vast network of traces rendering all the parts of my body unreachable by language or reason or any of the other consolations we use to avoid confronting the absence of logic; there are no divisions between language and the body other than those we create in our need for dissolution: I am not these words these words are not me not mine not his not ours they do not even belong to themselves... how then can we trust them, these perpetrators of Chinese whispers in the small hours that renege on their promises and leave us no less guideless and unsure in their presence than in their absence? But for now, as I lie here suspended and weightlessly joined to you, these words that circumnavigate my flesh take on the appearance of the sweetest embrace.

Jj

In another place, at another time, the structure of society was such that these two men would find a way of communicating by which the elder passed on his knowledge to the younger. A certain tutelage would bind them, and the price of this bond would be the flesh; the pucker of the young man's anus would yield to the hardened tip of the older man's penis and, spittle-slicked, the firmness would puncture and slide in right up to the dark-haired root.

Giving knowledge and giving pleasure, taking knowledge and taking pleasure. These exchanges are lost now, this particular form of libidinal economy confused, worn out, meaningless. Instead, these two men sit next to each other on the sofa and the older man listens to the younger man speak. He tells him that his grandfather is dying, that he has been awake all night at the hospital. His voice is soft and lethargic, revealing no emotion or energy. Bored; his voice is bored. In the same uncertain monotone, he starts to talk about his favourite novels, which are all about serial killers. In one of them, a serial killer called the Birdman puts a live bird in the hollowed-out ribcage of his victims. He recounts a short story he is writing, about a female serial killer who cuts the fingers off a man she has just killed and masturbates with one of them.

Seventeen and thirty-seven. There seems, to the older man, a curious symmetry to their ages. He begins to recall what he was like at seventeen, not listening much to the boy's quiet mumble, but letting memories arise from the dark still waters he polices more and more these days. Some numerologist might unearth patterns in these two numbers, some cosmic link, some cabbalistic augury or message. But not me.

'My teacher really liked the story,' the boy mutters, 'but she said she wouldn't like to pay my psychiatric bills.' His eyes are a clear, clean, glassy blue, fringed with long dark lashes. Surrounded by books most of which he has read, the older man can think of nothing to say.

The silence that has fallen between them is fragile enough to be broken by the move of a hand. A simple gesture, such as the younger man sliding his hand across the older man's thigh and letting it rest there. The older man responds by standing up and pulling the curtains closed, blocking out the late afternoon light. He sits back down and the hand returns to his thigh, sliding up to cup his stiffening crotch. Awkwardly, their mouths now meet; the older man is shocked by the softness of the boy's face, and an image unfolds of the last time he kissed a woman. All of his life seems to scurry for cover under the tenderness of that beardless kiss. As their clothes are removed, the boy grows more animated.

His lethargy, or shyness, diminishes as his nakedness increases. His lips are now circled with red from the older man's stubble, his face open and radiant with need. The face unnerves me: I have seen it before, in a dream or a past life, or a memory since erased.

If there is an exchange of knowledge here, in amongst the kissing and the licking and the sucking, it eludes them both, and after the deed is done they part none the wiser – or perhaps I am being unfair; perhaps there is something that each one takes away, like a prize, something to be kept and occasionally viewed as a reminder of what was achieved on that winter afternoon when their lives didn't change, even though, in truth, they never expected them to.

If desire is repressed it is because every position of desire, no matter how small, is capable of calling into question the established order of society.

Kk

Into the depths of the shrubbery in Finsbury Park, on a warm, orangey-blue-skied summer night, I followed you. The greenblack trees seemed to part as you led me to a derelict scout hut, its outside walls pebbledashed with chips of moonlight, its windows paneless, filled with yellow veils of candlelight and the uncertain sway of shadows. The sound of voices reached us from inside. You moved closer and leaned in the window, and I did too, to notice that the floor was scattered with a forest of nightlights, radiating enough light to show us a group of four or five men sitting and drinking and smoking and talking amongst a debris of newspapers and cans, rubbers and fag-ends. You waved at one of them and he called out a hello.

'Look what the cat's dragged in!' hissed a young boy in a white top, hood up, huddled over a beer can. 'Is that your trade, love? Bring him here, let's 'ave a proper look.'

You hopped with ease into the room, a graceful movement perfected on other nights like this, and I clambered through for the first time, apprehensive and thrilled.

'How many cocks you 'ad so far tonight?' Hooded Top asked.

'None,' you said, leaving a pause before adding, 'Yet,' and looking at me.

Hooded Top turned his face to me, 'You don't wanna touch her, luv. She's got every disease known to mankind.' And the group let out a gaggle of laughter.

A limit is not an origin: a limit requires no origin.

'Yeah,' chipped in another, 'she should carry a government health warning, that one!'

'Shut it,' you said, with a laugh in your voice, cracking open the can that someone had handed you. You took a long swig and handed it to me.

'Well, I haven't had one sniff of decent cock all night. It's fucking dead out there,' Hooded Top remarked. 'Where'd you find this one?' He looked me up and down.

'Over by the tennis courts,' you said.

'Nice,' Hooded Top said, looking at me.

The unconscious is an orphan; it produces itself within the identity of nature and man.

Then, picking up a nightlight and holding it to my face, he said, 'Very nice.' He put the light down and said, 'I'm telling you, you don't wanna be bothering with her, love, she's got the tiniest cock you ever laid eyes on. You should see mine, though. I've got a right whopper, I have.'

'Come on,' you said, grabbing my hand, 'I'll show you around.'

'No!' shrieked Hooded Top. 'We've not finished decorating yet! The place is a right fuckin' state!'

You smirked, and led me through a doorway blacker than the mouth of hell. 'Have fun!' someone yelled after us.

We find the freedom to choose, in the firefull moment, between an endless series of possible selves.

You led me into other rooms thick with a darkness that allowed no vision at all, so that as we ventured away from the others we could make out less and less of our surroundings. You flicked on your lighter and led me down a short hallway off which other rooms led, all with their doors hanging off, or kicked in. Language is embodied. In the bathroom your lighter flame illuminated the knuckled ceramic white of a toilet bowl. Everywhere rubble crunched underfoot. You led me into a larger room at the back of the building, where two men were fucking by a window. You doused the lighter. A series of grunts and sighs scurried across the room towards us. We moved nearer to them, till we could see their phosphorescent flesh and smell the amyl and rubber aura that surrounded them.

The personal material of transgression does not exist prior to the prohibition. In other words, transgression is creative.

You rubbed the front of my jeans and I rubbed the front of yours. The guy getting fucked gestured for us to move closer and you stood in front of him and unbuttoned your fly, feeding him your stiff cock. You gestured to me to move closer and I did, removing my own cock and offering that to his eager mouth. You kissed me, your hands roaming, and your eyes were staring straight into mine and when you dropped me a wink our joy lit up the room and you so close, your cock pushed up against mine inside this stranger's mouth, your arm around my shoulder. And the guy fucking leaned across and joined in with our kiss, and the three of us sucked and slurped on each other's tongues and the guy getting spitroasted let out a stream of muffled moans that reverberated down our cocks and up into our tongues, describing a circuit that shook all four of us where we stood like bolts of electricity through a lunatic's daydreams. This is the way the world begins, in the instance of an instant that can never be recalled except anaemically so that the desire for desire becomes a desire for immediacy even in the face of impossibility until the moment when the moment when the moment becomes both less than itself and more than itself at the same time and the body chooses to reach out and touch it as it passes that moment of time and it is a touch such a touch of tongue brain cock arse such a touch that the moment is able to relive itself and never stop never stop and reflect only move towards that is the point only move towards the point that is coming that comes that is coming that comes that came that has gone: the eternal is present in an atom of duration.

must have a body because some obscure object lives within me.

Ruby, who in a former life was Rudy, running around with his Chelsea hooligan mates kicking nine bells out of anyone and everyone, is telling us about her latest trade. Ruby has yet to have the chop the op and finds plenty of men who want to suck on a cock in a frock. She is regaling us as we stand by the moonblue trees, having a break from the relentless hunt for satiety, performing for us the monologue with which she accompanied her last conquest. She is dressed to depress, in a black strappy number that shows off the scars where the British Bulldog and Union Jack tattoos have been removed; she stands there, cross-eyed with drink in a cross-eyed wig, yelling: 'Oh, yeah, go on, baby, suck on my gonorrhoea, suck on my AIDS, suck on my herpes, yeah, suck it, suck my syphilis, go on, suck my AIDS, go on, suck it, suck my gonorrhoea, suck my herpes, suck my fucking AIDS.' She waits for the laughter to die down before adding, 'And you know what, the bastard wouldn't even swallow.'

Now and again Rudy makes an appearance, and Ruby's feminine demeanour disappears in a vapour of violence. She builds such walls around herself that no one could ever scale them. But I have also seen that moment when who she wants to be and who she appears to be coincide so gloriously that it is enough to make you trust in saints.

It is thus not a question of language or the body, but language *and* the body as an interface of matter itself.

Mm

A wasteland.

Bald earth sprouting a comb-over of weeds.

Night-time.

A suburb somewhere in Southern Italy.

A man I have just met is fucking me over the bonnet of his car, which is parked in a pathway swathed between an overgrown field and a dense orchard, beyond which the only indication of civilisation is the howling of a pack of dogs. The stars and the sound of the cicadas knit a blanket around me, and the metal against my skin is still warm from the engine. His friend has his cock in my mouth and thrusts unenthusiastically, more taken by the sight of his mate's cock slamming into me, a sight he illuminates with a torch that he holds and guides like a spotlight. They chatter away to each other in Italian (a language I don't speak) and behave, for all the world, as though I weren't there. The present no longer has any meaning. I am merely a sensation suspended between them, an excuse for a commonality each, perhaps, in his own silent way, craves – but could never, except now, with my flesh shared like a meal between them, even begin to articulate. These visions of excess burn brightest.

Nn

A dream about you.

Its appearance, furthermore, provokes both fear and fascination.

I was in a record shop when suddenly there appeared before me a naked man who so corresponded with my desire that it was as unsettling as a dream come true. He wanted me to wash him and as I did – people all around still rifling through records – I realised, with a joy that also broke my heart with its impossibility, its fragility and its immateriality, that it was you. I washed your body slowly, tenderly, my heart speeding away: so happy it hurt. When I had finished, I stood up, and our eyes met for the first time, followed by our mouths. To kiss you again made me weak and afraid, but so happy. So happy. Then you told me you had a lover, and he appeared beside you, also naked. He doesn't speak English, you said. I told you that I too have a lover and I turned around to him. I put my arm across his shoulders. It is clear to both you and me, without a word being spoken, that we want each other as much as we ever did. Your eyes, my eyes, our eyes. Our bodies like two strange angels, calling to each other in a frequency outside of human range. It must be the saddest sound. I'm glad that we can't hear it. It would never stop breaking our hearts. The difference between what we want and what we are able to do emerges with the slow, poisonous crawl of grief. The hunger doesn't abate, it seems; it only eats you up.

I wake to find your presence still alighting on my skin, a fragment of your warmth, the weight of you still pressing, and a blurred memory of the dream's end. The skin thus functions as an epistemological limit, even in the most phantasmatic journeyings beyond it.

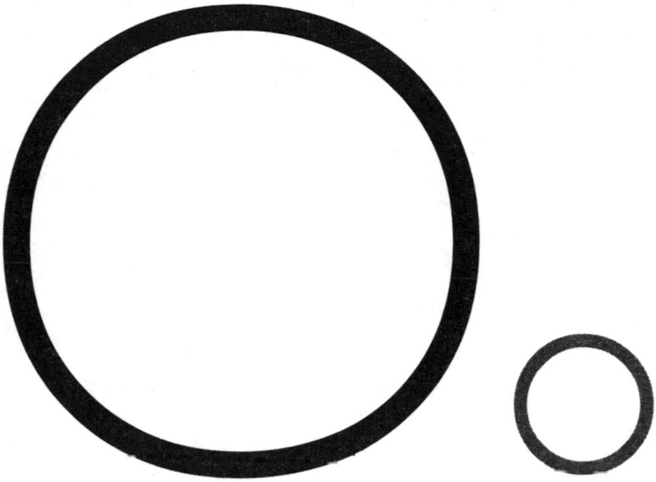

The house was in need of repair, and looked as if it hadn't been lived in for a while. I think he only used it for such encounters. He offered us warm fizzy white wine to drink. The house smelled of dereliction and suspended existences. There were several dogs, of varying sizes and breeds, all yapping and barking as if they had something important to impart. In one room the floor was covered in dry dog food knocked from a zigzag of bowls. We went to the bedroom and me and my mate started to undress the guy and kiss him. My friend got the guy's cock out practically straight away, and thank god it was a decent size. We both sucked it for a while and it grew bigger and bigger till we were both impressed and excited. After a while we were all naked and the guy wanted to fuck me. So he fucked me and I watched in the dressing table mirror.

Where do they come from, these voices that tell us what to do?

When we'd finished, and my friend had swallowed the guy's spunk, we got dressed. My mate didn't want the man to put his cock away. He held onto it and couldn't stop kissing it and saying, 'Wow! It's gorgeous.' He was totally in love with it.

In this society I live in, everyone dreams of being able to speak like this. But it really isn't possible to speak like this in our society. If sexuality has a voice it has yet to find it.

Pp

He walks in the door and falls straight to the floor, belly pressed against the boards, and begins slurping from the dog bowl of piss you have placed there. He breaks off to look up at you and ask, 'Does sir want me to drink it all?'

'Yes.'

You marvel at his submission, at his desire to be degraded. It fascinates and disgusts you. Short-term memory includes forgetting as a process.

You pull down your football shorts and pull aside your jockstrap, releasing your semi-hard cock, and then you watch him kneel at your feet and hold the bowl up to his mouth so he can drain it – with a delicacy that belies the moment – in tiny bird sips.

'Good boy,' you say when he has finished and placed the bowl back down.

You push your cock into his mouth, right down to the root, making him gag and choke, which makes you harder. You withdraw and slap your prick against his face, and he groans. You turn around, and present your rump to his face. He buries his foraging tongue, as if he could crawl inside and sleep on the moss there, die there.

The veneration I feel for that part of the body and the great tenderness that I have bestowed on the men who have allowed me to enter it, the grace and sweetness of their gift, oblige me to speak of all this with respect. It is not profaning the most beloved of the dead to speak, in the guise of a poem whose tone is still unknowable, of the happiness he offered me when my face was buried in a fleece that was damp with my sweat and saliva and that stuck together in little locks of hair which dried after love-making and remained stiff.

You turn around and hold out your cock, uttering the single word, 'Toilet.'

He holds his mouth open for the steady jet of warm, clear liquid, which arcs from your body to his, from inside you to inside him, this circuit of pleasure and waste that constructs its own economy within this blasted region of the soul.

By the time he leaves, he has choked so much on your cock that bile stains are visible on his shirt and trousers, you can see the black curls of his chest hair through the damp fabric; he has drunk your piss and swallowed your cum, and thanked you for the privilege. He measures the success of these encounters by the amount of piss and seed consumed.

Something has been released, some demon fed; the walls fall away and spaces yawn around you, unfathomable, unknowable spaces. And although it is still daylight, all you can see is darkness, the many shades of darkness, patterning your vision of yourself and this world, yourself in this world. And you see him, getting into his car, renegotiating his way back into his life, as you must renegotiate your way back into yours. It isn't possible to write sufficiently in the name of an outside.

Qq

The bed is covered in naked men, an eiderdown of flesh. Two Italians (one from the north, one from the south), a Brazilian, and two Brits (one from the north, one from the south).

Commenting on the action later to a friend, one of them will say, 'I took two cocks up my arse at once; it felt fucking great,' thereby proving the inadequacy of words, demonstrating how they wring dry the intensity of every moment and hang it up for inspection, hang it out to dry, colourless and mistaken. Wrap me in colours that cannot be described, patterns that change with each movement like a kaleidoscope. Give me a world beyond what is here. Give me a body in flames dancing in a place where there is no shame. Give me lies, if you like, but take me there, to that other world where language can only play games of hide and seek with what is really going on.

Either that or give me the words with which I can speak, teach me a new tongue that licks itself closer to the contours of bodies. Make my voice form shapes and sounds approximating more perfectly the perfect anguish of my joy. How does anybody learn? How can language say that? It trips and flies like an angel avoiding the bullets being shot at its feet. A dance of desperation and avoidance. Give me words with substance, words that taste of skin and smell like a well-fucked man. Give me a new alphabet, a new vocabulary of sliding verbs and solid nouns. A is for all of it, B is for bareback, C is for craving. Twenty-six letters burning in the flames like a taste upon the tongue. D is for deeper, E is for everything, F is for fear. And fear is for those who cannot speak this way, but stutter none the less, tripping over tongues that hold a key, a key to another world, a key that is swallowed before it can be snatched and used to unlock the cage door, before it can let loose this new alphabet that would flit around your head like so many birds, embroidering a song with no meaning, a song that exists for its own sake, for its own beauty, a song that tells of nothing but the joy it manifests.

Give me this language, if you can.

Rr

You press the buzzer and the black door releases with a click. On your left immediately as you enter: a doorway, leading to a badly lit room. You walk into it and approach a counter where a portly man with a grey ponytail and beard greets you.

'That'll be five pounds, dear,' he says, and you hand over the folded note in your hand. The act of submission, in other words, is linked to the very process by which knowledge is acquired.

You then remove your jacket and swap it for the ticket another man is holding out to you. You feel a mixture of emotions, lust mingled with fear, inhibition fighting courage and curiosity, and gradually losing. Your thoughts tumble and dance, a mixture of memories and fantasies, lighting the fuse, lighting your way.

You turn and look around, taking in the vintage porn-mag collage papering most of the walls and the timelessness it seems to create. In one corner, an L-shaped unit of cushioned seating, on which a topless man is sitting, rolling a spliff. A television screen shows a silent moving image of men having sex. You see a cock slide into an eager mouth as you make your way to the door on your right, a door through which you walk to find a staircase leading down. You descend into the Sybarite's cave – a cellar divided into rooms, all of which have bare, black walls licked with condensation. You can smell amyl nitrate spit sweat and semen blended into some odour you recognise. It is hot, and it takes a while for your eyes to adjust to the darkness. A man wearing nothing but a jock strap and army boots passes you, exchanging a glance.

You follow him into a room with a bench running along two walls, upon which sits a naked man, sucking off the man standing before him. In another corner a crowd of men are gathered around a man on his knees, taking it in turns to feed him their cocks. Your ears fill with the deep slow lowing of the pleasured. You pass through this room and find yourself in front of a doorway, curtained off with a black piece of cloth. *A season, a winter, a summer, an hour, a date have a perfect individuality lacking nothing, even though this individuality is different from that of a thing or a subject.* You push aside the curtain and enter the darkroom. You can hear the sounds of slurping and sighing, gagging and groaning unfolding in the darkness around you. The familiar sounds lash around you like the ropes that held Odysseus. Hands are unbuttoning your jeans, easing out your cock and you feel lips around it. Within seconds you are rock-hard, tuned in to every sensation. You reach out your hands and find a cock in the darkness, seeing with your fingertips its dimensions, its girth. Your hands explore your surroundings, the bodies in your vicinity. You select the one you want and move towards it, withdrawing from a mouth unwilling to release its prey.

Stories must contain things that are not simply replacements, but concrete individuations that have a status of their own and direct the metamorphosis.

That is how we need to feel.

You fall to your knees before your chosen prize and anticipate the feeling, the taste, a second before it becomes reality, unlocking doors into your soul. Nothing else exists for you but this throatful ease. Hands caress your hair, as you caress his furred, tense buttocks.

This is the way the world ends. Annihilation of the self is so close to pleasure as to make no difference. This is the way your world ends. You enter this new life with its fog of joy and intensity. You groan as you become something else, something not quite human, some dark hybrid hanging somewhere between man and beast, some creature nothing and no one can ever fully tame; and this realisation, this transformation, always leaves in its wake, always, every time, that unnameable feeling of a werewolf showing remorse for those he has slain and devoured. By claiming the existence of 'innocent' monsters, the poet-narrator is thus securing for himself an exoneration from blame or guilt: he cannot help his passion, his fascination, his curiosity.

Ss

There are places only the night knows, places only shadows can show us. The city wears a different face when darkness falls, a face I prefer. I walk the occluded streets looking for something, looking for something, looking for something. A knowledge of the shadow, that eats away at logic, creating patterns far brighter than I can bear; patterns that burn at the temperature of wanting. It traces its way through my veins, this wanting, finding solace only when I fall and feast. I find solace only when I fall and feast. This map I draw with the tip of my tongue takes refuge in a book of dreams. Forgive me for not having the words to describe it, this place in which I dwell. I have tried, I have tried. I have drenched myself in words and sensations, seeking a way to make them speak to one another. This is all I have to offer.

The body wants what it wants. The chaos of the body's wants – as we know – will never surrender itself to language, can never succumb to reason, even if, even if, even if it wanted to – which it never will. Words will help you to live, as your body will help you to die. When the body lets go, the mind lets go too. And fear is the least part, that's what I learnt first.

I know I fly, like Icarus, too close to the sun; I feel its heat on my wings. But I also know that only this white-hot danger can ever bring me peace. As the wax softens and gives I feel the height more keenly; the altitude, the drop, entice me like a siren song: oblivion, waiting to enfold me.

T†

Movements, becomings, in other words pure relations of speed and slowness, are below and above the threshold of perception. Nothing left but the zigzag of a line, like the lash of the whip of an enraged cart driver shredding faces and landscapes.

I am hanging, suspended, like an angel trapped in the branches of a tree, sling-shot and low-slung; the cum of twenty men drips from me, like hot wax, creating a pool beneath me on the pearl-licked floor. I hang like a cage between heaven and earth, inside which, perched on a swing, my big red heart is singing. The taste of twenty men bruises my lips. I suffocate in an aroma composed of sweat and amyl and the cold damp of bare brick. I am euphoric with weightlessness, lost in some transcendence that still defies language, try as I might to trap it in the loose-knit net language offers. Each grunt still rings in my ear, each thrust still lodges in the archive of my skin. Each touch and taste documented, etched with crystal on the cold metal of my memory. Every detail hovers above the moment like a halo: the leather encasing my back, the metal links kissing my legs, the circuit of pleasure flickering around me like static, the solidity of the last cock inside me.

And still... still I want more, still I feel a need within that nothing can assuage, a deep, dark thirst or hunger that comes from some place I have yet to find. Perhaps I never will. Perhaps this maze inside me leads nowhere at all. I am raw from the roaring of my soul, for tonight my evil twin stormed the city gates and besieged me.

I am pure sensation, no consciousness, no ego. Pure id: still demanding, still hankering.

The claims society makes on the body will, perhaps, always be at odds with the claims the body makes on itself. As I reach for my clothes, still stoned from the experience, still wobbly, and proceed to dress, I find the pieces of that other self I left behind in the scramble to obey my every wish. I wrap my self around me like a life. I retrieve the fragments of another individual and assume the shape they offer. For now I can inhabit the oblivion, like an addict after a fix, a cloud around my head that will rain down happiness. Everything on earth is broken apart by vibrations of various amplitudes and durations. Each moment is as empty or as full as a mirror.

U u

I am oblivion, I recognise no law, belong to no one, but all belong to me. I move towards a darkness only I can see or feel. I am that which can never be caught, never delivered, that crawls between bodies, towards the new night that promises to be glorious, festooned with wounded males, praying for rack and ruin.

As the sun is setting I step off the train at an unknown station in Essex, make my way outside and climb into the passenger seat of a silver BMW, and this man I am meeting for the first time, let's call him R, greets me. Handsome, stocky, rough. As we pull out of the car park he places my hand on his crotch, and I know I am in for a good time. After five minutes, we pull into the gravel drive of a large detached house. In the driveway stand two ice-cream vans. Once inside, we begin to kiss and before long I am kneeling with his glorious prick in my mouth. He pulls back the foreskin and I can taste the fat head. We swap places. He stands and opens the fridge door, pulling out a can of lager and handing it to me.

'Drink,' he says, 'I'll be wanting your piss later.'

In the intellectual representations in circulation, pleasure is reduced to a concession; in other words, it is reduced to a diversion whose role is subsidiary.

Pleasure is expenditure; we exchange kisses that chew at flesh and lick at teeth, drawing sighs and some kind of sweetness from deep within. We create an economy of pleasure. He dribbles spittle into my mouth. I drink it. We move to the bedroom and strip and climb onto the bed. I nuzzle the fur on his chest and release a groan. This is a great place to be. I hold it, this place, for as long as I dare. (In many ways, I have yet to let go, even now, all these years later. The combined sensation of his fuzzy chest against my face and his hard cock pressed against my stomach still hovers somewhere just underneath my skin. It would take nothing, a mere thought or gesture, as now, for me to conjure it and hold it again. The memory is a gift I cherish.)

He gets up and goes into the lounge, returning with a small plastic box from which he removes a blue diamond-shaped pill. He snaps it in two with his teeth and hands me one half, which I swallow with a swig of beer. He necks the other himself, swallowing without beer. He holds out his open palm and I lick up the white tablet that lies in it. He swallows his and we come together again in kisses that say all we need to say. It is raining outside. It has been raining all day. I can feel it on my skin. It dissolves me. It washes away all anxiety as it soaks through to the marrow, making my body disappear completely, leaving me naked, vulnerable as happiness itself. Half an hour later, we break for a cigarette – at least, I smoke, and then place my lips upon his and blow the grey fumes into his mouth.

Like the anus, the mouth is a site at which the dispersion of the body's drives and instincts becomes concentrated, crystallised, and dangerously pleasurable.

He inhales, taking the smoke deep within his lungs, throwing back his head and closing his eyes as the diluted smoke shoots out of his nostrils. With the tip of my tongue I trace a line from the hollow of his neck to the nub of his chin.

'Second-hand smoke tastes so good,' he says with a white grin. Chaos and calm: it seems sometimes that all of my life has been spent shuttling between those two emotions, the one pushing the other like a magnetic pole until some kind of brief, momentary harmony between the two forces is achieved, only to be broken in a split second which tilts me back again to one or the other. It exhausts me, this battle, but such exhaustion has a compulsion all its own that draws me towards it nevertheless, like seeking transient reprise in a hurricane's eye.

This exchange, from my lungs to his, this rope of smoke that encircles our spirits like a garland – this is what I came for.

Vv

You tell me you want to lick your boyfriend's cock while he fucks me. You tell me you don't often get to see your boyfriend fuck someone. You are as excited as a child on Christmas morning. I am on my hands and knees, impaled so deeply by your boyfriend's cock that it seems like he has penetrated the entire length of my spine. The tension unravels and my rectum flickers around the solidity of him, responding to its presence in waves of muscular pulsion as we fall into the rhythm of each other. I can hear you both breathing behind me. I can feel your face against my buttocks as you lick him. You are so excited by this that you come, all across my back, loudly howling and barking your immense pleasure. Later you explain that the first time you had sex with a man was in a cave by the sea, and once you were inside the cave five fishermen in their boats set up just outside the cave's entrance, so you both had to come without a sound. Ever since, you tell me, you have these occasional intense orgasms that tear themselves out of you like a birth, leaving you fragile and bereft. It's like a near-death experience, you explain, and one day, you are convinced, it will kill you. This little death – this savagery that tears us momentarily from our bodies – will one day gather up its strength and fell us. Just as no man can know another's death, so we each remain isolated in our pleasure, this delicate shell of nerve-endings acting like a barrier, a boundary, against which the world dissolves. The soul is made of the same stuff as ghosts, after all. It haunts our bodies, ranging through the empty, dusty rooms of the flesh looking for a mate, and, finding none, imagines itself alone, when in truth, in the next room, breathing stirs the embers: existence toiling like a beast on all fours against the dissolution of personal identity.

We are waiting for another man to arrive, whom we'll call S. S arrives, and he is taller than me, stockier, shaved head, pleasant face, and almost immediately R has pulled down S's trackpants to reveal a thick, cut, semi-hard nine-incher, which he proceeds to suck into full splendour. I watch from the couch, loving the sight, until R gestures me over and I kneel beside him, and he feeds me S's cock. The chemicals are kicking in now and knocking down all my reserve like a bull at a gate. S's cock feels so good. I take it right down to the thick root until it fills me entirely. The surrounding presence of wounded males is already a blessing that is granted me in this festival of inner calm. I suppose I could describe the combinations of bodies, the interactions of sensation, the way R and I take turns riding S's huge hard cock, the sight of R draining a pint glass of my clear beery piss – I could try and capture that, somehow, I suppose. I could try to find words that might inscribe the warm outlines of our intensity, but how can you draw a line around a flame, around the molten heat of my orgasm – R working my arse with the thickest black rubber cock and S pushing his prick deeper down my throat? Deep within my body the tip of S's cock touches the tip of the dildo, and a blue bolt snaps between them like a synapse.

Erotic play discloses a nameless world, which is revealed by the nocturnal language of lovers. Such language is not written down. It is whispered into the ear at night, but by dawn it has been forgotten. The kisses the three of us shared cannot be shared. They are from a world only we inhabited; a land of dark and innocent pleasures, a land that could sustain us with its natural resources if it weren't so ripped and torn and plagued with insanity. The land of a joy only shadows can know and taste. It cannot be demonstrated, cannot be shown, except at the point of its own rupture, its own disappearance.

Xx

In the blue-licked curves of a shoreline cave, saltwater lapping at their thighs, two naked men stand, prick to prick, so sweet, locked in a clinch that craves. Their ascent to the summits of pleasure marks the beginning of time: this is the way the world begins. In shadows and heat, in caves where silence echoes. On hitting the water, their sperm turns into a shoal of silvered fish that swims around their calves, sparkling like tiny lights and plucking kisses from the sweet flesh.

This a world I will never know, and this is a world I defend. Language makes the soul possible, yet every statement we make remains a betrayal. This is the way the world begins. Like a dream we try to locate and unpick, these emotions unravel their wares. It remains like a sensation, like a memory, this other life, rippling beneath my skin, turning me into a beam of light as it cuts through a wave.

Yy

Fascination is a process by which we are pulled further away from reason, and thus it threatens to destabilise the world as something known.

A shaft of sunlight picks out the smooth whiteness of a man's naked body through the trees, reclined on a towel spread over the grey of a gravestone. He's playing with his semi-hard cock and, as I stand observing, another man approaches him and lowers his open mouth onto it. I walk on, down the narrow, angular pathways, not knowing quite what I am looking for until I find it. How it will arrive, and what it will look like, are unknown to me as yet, and the mystery fuels the search. The summer sun is hot as I pass through patches of it breaking between the trees in bright flickers of light. I want everything. The freedom and the guile. I don't want to leave here without it.

In this place of the dead we bring ourselves to life, our seed enriching this soil, these feral shadows. We scratch and claw amidst the undergrowth like animals and we rut and rut, locked into a present we want to sustain. The frenzy, perhaps, comes from knowing we can't. It ends.

It ends. And even now you're miles away, boxing with your absurd shadow. Does the body reconcile us to death or does it provide a diversion from it? And these places we find, these arbitrary places of furtive pleasure, what kind of map do they draw? All this I am, and I want to be: at the same time dove, serpent, and pig.

Zz

We need a thinking that does not fall apart in the face of pleasure, a self-consciousness that does not steal away when it is time to explore possibility to the limit.

I made so much noise when I came that you asked if I was all right. This disembodied voice from behind the door. For twenty minutes you'd sucked me into a frenzy, an infinity, a place I cannot name. And the anonymity breaks, a subjectivity emerges from behind the sensation of cock and mouth, beyond the noise you pulled from me, like a lifeguard hoisting a drowner from a pool.

'I'm fine,' I said.

The door has graffiti on it, some primitive drawing of a spurting cock. It keeps me both inside your flat and outside your flat at the same time. I am in the hallway, at the top of a flight of stairs. Behind me, the wall is adorned with camouflage netting. Techno music bleeds from behind the door in which two holes have been cut and curtained with black fabric. I seek pleasure. I seek the nerves under my skin. The narrow pathway; the layers; the scroll of ancient hieroglyphs.

If identification is a nomination, a designation, then simulation is the writing corresponding to it, writing that is strangely polyvocal, flush with the real. Desire is part of the infrastructure.

Beyond the anonymity, our separate lives spin their own particular courses, going to people and places we will never share, or never know. In this thought – perhaps – lies at least part of the pleasure, expressed directly in those sounds that ripped from me. This body is stolen. This simple world becomes too much. These limbs are not my limbs.

The section entitled 'P' contains a quotation from Jean Genet's novel, *Funeral Rites*, translated by Bernard Frechtman, New York: Grove Press, 1969, p.21.

Section 'R' includes a quotation from Gilles Deleuze and Félix Guattari's *A Thousand Plateaus: Capitalism and Schizophrenia*, translated by Brian Massumi, Minneapolis: University of Minnesota Press, 1993, p.288.

Acknowledgements

The biggest love to my family, and to my Benjamin.

To my agent, Adrian Weston, and the team at Myriad Editions – Candida Lacey, Vicky Blunden, Corinne Pearlman, Linda McQueen and Emma Dowson – I owe everything. This text is what it is thanks in particular to Vicky and Linda's skilled eyes, creative insight and patient hearts.

To my fabulous, loyal and indulgent friends, especially Michael Atavar, Darius Amini, Abigail Bamsey, John Lee Bird, Alex Black, Helen Boulter, Pippa Brooks, George Cayford, Matthew Fennimore, Lucien Gouiran, Sally Gross, Hally, Wendyl Harris, Alexis Joshua, Louise Lambe, Sadie Lee, Clayton Littlewood, James Maker, David Male, Steve Muscroft, Joe Pop, Clive Reeve, Chris Rose, Stephane Sionville, Matthew Stradling, Justin Ward, Sue Smallwood, Roy Woolley. Huge love to Mich Jamieson and David Hoyle.

To Jim MacSweeney and Uli Lenart at Gay's the Word, the best bookshop in the world, where I first read some of these pieces in public.

An extract from this work appeared in *The Everyday Experiment: Sampling the design, the queer and the politics in the everyday*, edited and published by Andrew Slatter, 2010.

If you liked *Twentysix*, you might like Jonathan Kemp's critically acclaimed début novel *London Triptych*.

For an exclusive extract, read on…

1954

I spent last night in a police cell.

Gore had taken me to my first queer pub, the Lord Barrymore, near Regent's Park. I've walked past it on several occasions, never imagining for a minute what it was, and not being a pub person I'd never had cause to go in. But last night we went for a drink there.

A few weeks ago, Gore was astonished to hear that I'd never been inside a queer pub. He refused even to believe me to begin with. Once I convinced him that it was true, he insisted the situation be rectified. I agreed to go to one with him. A few weeks went by and nothing more was said about it. But yesterday, I brought the subject up and asked whether he was free that evening. He said yes, so after our meal we got a cab into town.

I felt a great deal of trepidation during the cab ride, and despite all the wine we'd drunk with our meal I was incredibly nervous as we entered. There was a lot of rococo carved glass over and behind the counter and a number of mahogany chairs with red leather upholstery. A fog of cigarette smoke blurred the air. Apparently it had only gone queer in the last few months; before that it was an ordinary public house. Gore informed me that once a place has become established as a queer pub, the police start raiding it on a regular basis so that the clientele have to move on to another pub.

There were about thirty people there when we arrived. All of them turned to look at us when we walked in. As we made our way to the bar I noticed Gore nod acquaintance to a few men and I wondered if any of them were his punters, but dismissed the thought. There were two or three young soldiers by the dartboard, and a clutch of young men standing by the fire who seemed to be wearing make-up, the paint illuminated by the firelight. The rest were an unremarkable and fairly typical crowd of men. I overheard bits of conversations as I followed Gore. Dog-ends, my mother used to call them.

'She said, "Well don't ask me, dear, I've only got two inches of vagina left."'

'So, by the time I finally got to Kathmandu…'

'If I catch you strolling and caterwauling I'll beat the milk out of your breasts, so I will.'

'Smell her!'

Gore ordered the drinks and I gave him the money to pay for them. As he took it, I noticed those around us watching the transaction, and knew how it must seem to them. A feeling of both pride and shame washed through me.

If only.

It was easy enough finding a seat, and Gore said it was because most people preferred to stand so they could observe everything, or rather everyone, in the room.

There didn't seem much to observe to me. Just a regular public house, except perhaps for the occasional shriek of hysterical laughter and the absence of women. I said as much to Gore when he returned with the drinks, and he explained that glances were being constantly exchanged and rendezvous being arranged without a word being spoken – an invisible web being spun around us of covert eye movements and facial gestures you'd be hard-pushed to notice. The soldiers, apparently, are well known for letting you fellate them in the gents', if you slip them a couple of quid.

Gore told me that the regulars call the landlord Mother. And in these places most of the punters are regulars. He explained that all eyes had been on us because they had never seen me before. I said I found the attention rather strange. He laughed, and I wasn't sure if he was laughing at me.

At that point, a grey-haired old man in an extremely tight burgundy velvet jacket and blue cravat, who had been staring and blinking at Gore ever since we'd sat down, came up to the table and grabbed Gore's hand. In the fruitiest voice, he said, '*Young man*, when *you* have a few spare hours and *I* have a few spare pounds of plaster of Paris, you *must* let me make a cast of your hands. They're divine.'

'Away with you, Jack!' Gore laughed, pulling his hand free.

'I'm serious, Gregory, I intend to immortalise them in bronze.' A lascivious grin spread across his face. 'And your cock too, if you'd let me.' He gave Gore a nudge.

'Behave,' Gore said, 'there'll be none of that talk in front of my friend here. He's an artist. A real artist.' Gore nodded in my direction.

Jack held out a limp hand for me to shake. 'Jack Rose.'

'Colin Read. Pleased to meet you.' I shook his hand.

'I knew an artist once,' he said.

'Sure you did, Jack, sure you did,' Gore teased, looking at me. 'Didn't you meet Mr Oscar Wilde himself, now?'

'No word of a lie,' he said, dropping the genteel accent and trowelling on the Cockney. 'I was a beautiful boy, not ashamed to say it, a shiny ripe apple in this veritable Eden, and Mr Wilde liked beautiful boys, as did all the swells that came my way. But we had something special, Mr Wilde and I. Treated me like gold, he did. Here, take a vada at this,' he said, plunging his hand into his inside jacket pocket and plucking out a tatty sepia photograph. He handed it over and said, 'Just you read what's written on the back of that, Mr Read, go on, read it. Aloud, if you don't mind.'

I read. '"*To Jack, my favourite writing desk, O. W.*"'

I said I was impressed, that I had enjoyed many of Wilde's writings.

'I had a silver cigarette case, too, what he gave me. But the filth took that.' He helped himself to a sip from my drink. 'It's a crime what this country did to that man, a crime!' he hissed.

Then without further encouragement he launched into a monologue. 'When they locked 'im up, London sank to its knees, five years before the century did, tatty and knackered, as grey as Victoria's hair. The inns were empty, the drag balls wiped off the face of the city like a tart's panstick. Most of the well-to-do queens had sodded off abroad, the ones who stayed too scared to play out their lust. The party was over. I fucked off up to Manchester, but I had such a miserable time I came back after a year. You ever been? Don't bother. I missed London. But the London I missed was no more.'

He paused for dramatic effect.

'But then,' he said, moving closer, 'ever so gradually, legions of Oscars started to spring up like flowers all over London, on every street corner in town from the Dilly to Oxford Street. So many Oscars. Vivid and proud.' His hands started to dance, stressing certain words with an invisible stitch of the smoky air. 'More timid than he had been, mind you, but taking their cue nevertheless from his former glory, before Lily Law kicked the living daylights out of him. And the resilience of this desire fascinated me. I heard the song of its voice and joined in the chorus. They were back: the taverns, and the drag parties, and the swells. You could suddenly make out a sparkle of gold feathers beneath the ash-grey pelt of London town.'

He paused, lost in some long-forgotten memory, a beatific smile lighting his wrinkled, powdered face. 'D'y'know, it was as if he had to die so as to be reincarnated not just as a person, but as a whole new century. That's how big he was.'

Then he turned to Gore and said, 'Can this old ponce ponce a vogue off you, duckie?' And while Gore was fishing in his jacket pocket Jack lifted Gore's glass and took a swig.

As Gore handed Jack a cigarette, there was a sudden burst of noise and half a dozen policemen crashed through the doors. Everybody froze. Absolute silence. My heart was racing. Jack just rolled his eyes as if to say, *here we go again*, and tilted forward to light his cigarette in the flame that Gore offered.

'Goodnight, sweet ladies,' Jack hissed before slinking off to the back of the room, gliding like a phantom.

'Good evening, gents,' said one of the policemen.

'How can we help you, officer?' asked the landlord.

'We're here to seek your co-operation.'

'Oh, yes?'

'If you'd all be so kind as to supply us with your names and addresses, then we'll be on our way.'

'Why?'

'Just procedure, sir.'

'But you've got them already. You were in here last week. There's nobody here tonight who wasn't here then. No one.' I looked at the floor.

'It won't take a minute, sir.'

Our table was nearest to the door and a policeman sat down in the seat Jack had vacated. I looked at Gore; he looked calm as anything.

'Evenin', ladies,' he said with an imbecilic grin. Neither of us spoke. 'If I could have your name, please, sir.'

'Gregory Moretti.'

'And where do you live, Mr Moretti?'

'With him,' he said, pointing at me. I couldn't believe my ears. I was confused as to why Gore would say that. But I didn't have much time to reflect on it, for the policeman turned immediately to me.

'Does he live with you, sir?'

'Yes,' I blurted out.

'You don't sound so sure, sir.'

'Yes, he does, he lives with me.'

'And what is your relationship with this young man, sir, if I may ask?'

I was momentarily flummoxed, and by the time I came out with 'friend' Gregory had already said 'son' the smallest fraction of a second faster.

The policeman closed his notepad, put away his pencil, stood up and asked us to accompany him to the station. I felt so humiliated I could hardly stand.

'Leave 'em alone, they've done no harm. Only having a bleedin' drink. It's not a crime,' yelled the landlord.

'Stay out of this, Mother.'

'Mr Wilson to you.'

They took us away in a Black Maria, and I felt as if I were being driven to my execution. Gore suddenly seemed like a complete stranger about whose life I knew absolutely nothing. To compound my humiliation, there were two men with us in the back of the van dressed in women's clothes, their faces covered in make-up. One of them explained that they'd just been arrested for soliciting in the park. They introduced themselves as Lady Godiva and Gilda Lily. Gilda did all the talking, explaining that Lady Godiva was still upset that the police had accosted her in the middle of a particularly enjoyable encounter, servicing a serviceman in possession of what Gilda termed 'the biggest cazzo in Christendom'. He leant across and said quietly, 'She takes her work too seriously, if you ask me.' He put a hand on my knee and said, 'There are two things I can't stand: size queens and small cocks.'

I looked at Lady Godiva. He looked at me and smiled weakly, exposing teeth so bucked I couldn't imagine anyone wanting to be fellated by him. My grandmother would have described them by saying he could eat an apple through a letterbox.

Gore and I exchanged not one word during the entire journey. The sounds of the traffic as we travelled through the city filled me with sadness. At the station we were separated immediately and taken into different rooms. I don't think I have ever been quite so petrified in my entire life. A police officer took down my details and then put me in a cell with Gilda and Lady Godiva, who still hadn't said a word. I was in there for what seemed hours. I wondered if they would interview me first and then Gore, or Gore first and then me, or both simultaneously, but concluded it didn't really matter. Our stories would not match. I wasn't about to start fabricating a life in which he was my son. Besides, what if he had decided to pretend he had simply used the wrong word accidentally in the pub and had meant to say friend? What if he was about to tell the truth? And what was the truth? Could I say he was a friend; could I lie and say he lived with me?

My mind was spinning with so many thoughts, and all the while Gilda was beside me recounting stories about the cock size of various members of parliament. 'They don't call them members for nothing, love, believe you me!' he roared.

And still the only torture was his absence.

I wondered what Gore was doing, why he hadn't been put in with us.

Finally, I was taken to an interview room, where I maintained that his current address was with me.

'Why did he say he was your son, do you think?' The policeman arched an eyebrow.

'I imagine he used the wrong word accidentally. He is multi-lingual and is prone to mistakes on occasion.'

'That's what he said.'

I relaxed a little.

'You know that the Lord Barrymore is frequented by homosexuals, do you, Mr Read?'

I said I did.

'And do you frequent the Lord Barrymore, Mr Read?'

I said that it was my first time there.

'It always is, sir, it always is.' He grinned and I was as tense as ever.

Then he pushed a sheet of text towards me and said, 'If you could just read through and sign this statement for me, Miss – sorry, *Mister* Read.' I read through it, considered pointing out the numerous errors in spelling, punctuation and grammar, but thought better of it. I signed it and pushed it back towards him and he declared me a free man.

'And Gregory?'

'He's waiting outside for you.' And he gave me that knowing grin again, and I thought to myself, *You don't know anything, you filthy Yahoo.* That was what my father used to say under his breath whenever anyone tried to talk to him whom he didn't like, which was almost everybody. I remember as a child thinking it a terrible name to call anyone. But, by Christ, that ape before me was a filthy Yahoo if ever I saw one. Where do they find them?

I found Gore skulking around outside, kicking the kerb like a naughty bored child.

'Come on,' I said, 'let's get home.' We took a black cab home in silence, and I found myself thinking about Frank Symonds sitting in all those cabs with all those boys years ago, and wondering what he might have talked to them about, or whether they too sat in a silence as deadly as this, like two creatures who had yet to develop a means to communicate. My mind was racing with words but none of them seemed the right thing to say. Not in front of a cabbie. As soon as we were in the house I asked Gore why he hadn't simply given his own address and he said he didn't have one. He told me he had run away from his place in Islington without paying his rent and is sleeping in parks or with friends. I told him that I was sorry about his situation, and would help as much as I could, but that there was absolutely no way he could stay here.

He laughed.

'Gore, this is no joking matter.'

I knew that, compared to the scrapes he'd regularly found himself in and the dangerous situations he'd placed himself in, a London bobby was child's play, but I still felt sick from the whole experience. I tried to keep a stern face but he carried on laughing and eventually I found myself succumbing to a smile and then I myself began to laugh. In some curious way I felt the experience had brought us closer, though God alone knows how or why. I was very cross with him, and he knew it, I could tell. I can't help feeling a little unsettled by the whole affair. Especially the police having my details. I imagine that they have a huge ledger in which they record the details of every homosexual they've ever unearthed, and I keep picturing the policeman who interviewed me scratching my name in it and blotting it dry with a grin of triumph. I thought of Montagu, Wildeblood and Pitt-Rivers in their cells. There but for the grace of God go I, I thought, even though I'm an atheist.

We were both in need of some sleep, so Gore took the couch and I took to my bed. Though I left my door open, he didn't take the hint. Just as well, for we were woken in the early morning by an almighty banging on the front door.